First published in the United States, Great Britain, Canada,
Australia, and New Zealand in 1993 by North-South Books,
an imprint of Nord-Süd Verlag AG, Gossau Zürich, Switzerland.

Distributed in the United States by North-South Books Inc., New York.

Library of Congress Cataloging-in-Publication Data
Scheidl, Gerda Marie.
[Gläserne Kugel. English]
The crystal ball / by Gerda Marie Scheidl ; illustrated by Nathalie Duroussy ;
translated by Rosemary Lanning.
Summary: After several attempts to solve the problem of the fierce giant
at the edge of their kingdom, a kind princess and a glassblower succeed in achieving peace.
ISBN 1-55858-197-9 (TRADE BINDING)
ISBN 1-55858-198-7 (LIBRARY BINDING)
[1. Fairy tales.   2. Giants—Fiction.]   I. Duroussy, Nathalie, ill.   II. Title.
PZ8.S2773Cr   1993
[E]—dc20   92-44762

British Library Cataloguing in Publication Data
Scheidl, Gerda Marie
Crystal Ball
I. Title   II. Lanning, Rosemary   III. Duroussy, Nathalie
833.914
ISBN 1-55858-197-9

1 3 5 7 9 10 8 6 4 2
Printed in Belgium

THE CRYSTAL BALL

BY Gerda Marie Scheidl

ILLUSTRATED BY Nathalie Duroussy

Translated by Rosemary Lanning

North-South Books

NEW YORK

THERE ONCE was a land where clear, sparkling rivers flowed through lush meadows dotted with groves of flowering trees. It was a beautiful place and the people who lived there should have been happy, but they were not. They lived in fear of a terrible giant who lived on the borders of their land, beyond the hills. No one had ever seen the giant, but on still, moonlit nights they could hear him roar.

Everyone was afraid, even the king in his castle. And his daughter, the princess, was so worried about what might happen that she fell ill.

"Something must be done," said the queen after she tucked the princess into bed.

"We must build an iron wall to keep the creature out," said the king's chief minister.

"Good idea," said the king. "Start work at once."

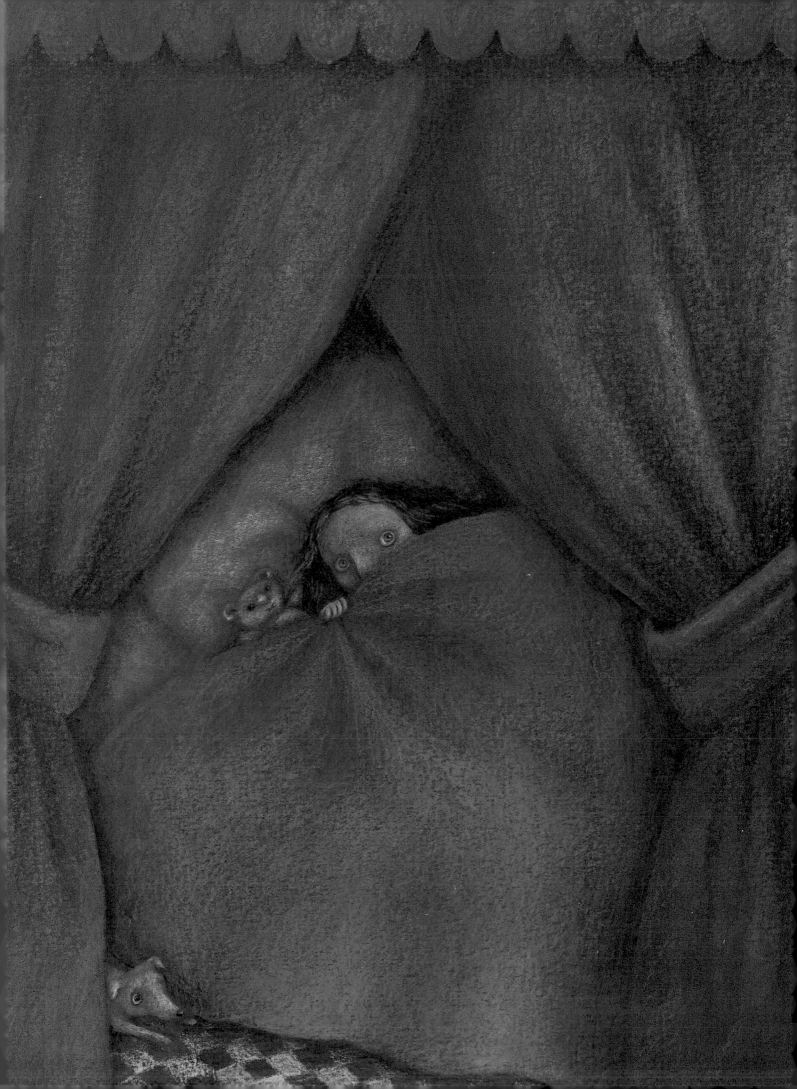

But when the princess saw what was happening, she pleaded with them to stop. "Look what the wall is doing to our beautiful land," she said.

The king looked, and saw that the meadows beside the wall were no longer lush, that trees in its path were being cut down and that the rivers had lost their sparkle. Clearly this was not the right thing to do. "But how else are we to protect ourselves?" he asked.

"Send a brave man to fight the horrible creature," said the queen.

The king sent out a proclamation: "If any man is brave enough to kill the giant, I will give him a roomful of gold."

The first person to come forward was a blacksmith. He held up a big sword and said, "I can kill anything with this."

"Go, then," said the king, "and free us from the terrible monster."

The blacksmith walked all the way over the hills until he came to a deep valley.

There he saw the giant.

The blacksmith tried to creep up on the terrifying creature, but it was no good. The giant had seen him coming. He seized the sword and snapped it in half.

"Going to kill me, were you?" he roared. "I wouldn't try that if I were you. Now go away before I kill you!"

With a yelp of fear, the blacksmith turned and ran back to the king. "Weapons are useless against such a monster," he wailed.

Then a rope maker stepped up.

"See this rope?" he said. "It's the strongest one I've ever made. I'll sneak up on the monster and tie its hands so tightly that it won't be able to move."

"Off you go, then," said the king.

Soon the rope maker came to the valley and saw the giant sitting quietly in the sun. Hiding in the trees, the man swung his rope and looped it over the giant's toe.

But the giant had seen the rope maker coming too. He tore the rope apart and bellowed, "Tie me up, would you? Go away, or I'll tie you up instead."

Gasping with fright, the rope maker ran back to the king. "No one's ever going to catch such a powerful giant," he said.

The princess looked very sad. "I'm sure you're doing this wrong," she said. "Why not try being nice to the giant? Take him a present, perhaps?"

"She's right," said the glassblower, coming through the castle door with a shimmering sphere in his hands. "Let me take him this crystal ball. When the giant holds this beautiful gift in his hands, surely he will see that I come as a friend."

So the glassblower went over the hills to find the giant. He walked right up to the enormous creature and held out the crystal ball. The giant drew back. Was this a weapon too? he wondered.

"Don't be afraid," said the glassblower. "The crystal ball is a gift from the king's daughter. She wants you and her father to be friends."

"Friends?" The giant laughed scornfully. "Until now, your king wanted only to kill me."

The glassblower smiled. "This is true," he said, "But that was because he was afraid. He thought you wanted to kill us."

The giant looked shocked. "Why would your king think such a thing?" he said.

"Because you are a giant," said the glassblower. "And everyone's afraid of giants, except me. Now please accept this ball as a sign of friendship."

The giant took the crystal ball and held it carefully in both hands. The ball began to glow, and its light spread out over the hills. As it did, a sweet melody could be heard. It sounded like a gentle call.

"They want us to come!" cried the princess. She ran out of the castle, and the king and queen and everyone else followed her.

When they found the giant, he was still gazing at the glowing ball.

Fearlessly the princess ran up to the giant.

"This is a beautiful gift," he said, "but I want you to look after it for me. Keep it in a place where everyone can see it. It will remind all of us that we must live peacefully together."

The giant let the crystal ball slip gently into her outstretched hands.

"I will," said the princess, clutching the ball. She sat on the giant's feet and smiled at the glassblower. They were proud of what they had accomplished. By working together, they had brought peace to the land.

As they sat gazing into each other's eyes, the townsfolk gathered in a circle around them, linked hands, and began a joyous dance to the melody of the crystal ball.